?/21

DESMOND COLE
GHOST PATROL

WHO WANTS I SCREAM?

by **Andres Miedoso**
illustrated by **Victor Rivas**

LITTLE SIMON
New York   London   Toronto   Sydney   New Delhi

LITTLE SIMON

An imprint of Simon & Schuster Children's Publishing Division

1230 Avenue of the Americas, New York, New York 10020

First Little Simon paperback edition July 2021

Copyright © 2021 by Simon & Schuster, Inc.

Also available in a Little Simon hardcover edition.

All rights reserved, including the right of reproduction in whole or in part in any form.

LITTLE SIMON is a registered trademark of Simon & Schuster, Inc.,

and associated colophon is a trademark of Simon & Schuster, Inc.

For information about special discounts for bulk purchases, please contact

Simon & Schuster Special Sales at 1-866-506-1949 or business@simonandschuster.com.

The Simon & Schuster Speakers Bureau can bring authors to your live event. For more information

or to book an event contact the Simon & Schuster Speakers Bureau at 1-866-248-3049 or

visit our website at www.simonspeakers.com.

Designed by Steve Scott

Manufactured in the United States of America 0621 MTN

2 4 6 8 10 9 7 5 3 1

Library of Congress Cataloging-in-Publication Data

Names: Miedoso, Andres, author. | Rivas, Victor, illustrator.

Title: Who wants I scream? / by Andres Miedoso ; illustrated by Victor Rivas.

Description: First Little Simon paperback edition. | New York : Little Simon, 2021. |

Series: Desmond Cole ghost patrol ; 14 | Summary: When the ice-cream man takes

a vacation during a very hot summer in Kersville, best friends Desmond and Andres

search for a substitute, with frightening results.

Identifiers: LCCN 2021007780 (print) | LCCN 2021007781 (ebook) |

ISBN 9781534499461 (paperback) | ISBN 9781534499478 (hardcover) | ISBN 9781534499485 (ebook)

Subjects: CYAC: Ice cream, ices, etc.—Fiction. | Supernatural—Fiction. |

Friendship—Fiction. | African Americans—Fiction. | Hispanic Americans—Fiction.

Classification: LCC PZ7.1.M518 Wh 2021 (print) |

LCC PZ7.1.M518 (ebook) | DDC [Fic]—dc23

LC record available at https://lccn.loc.gov/2021007780

LC ebook record available at https://lccn.loc.gov/2021007781

CONTENTS

CHAPTER ONE

Ice-Cream Headache

Let me tell you what you already know: Kids love ice cream!

Am I right?

I mean, there are *so* many flavors. You could have chocolate chip, double chocolate swirl, or even *triple* chocolate fudge.

There's strawberry cream, black-berry chunk, and blueberry brownie. And don't forget cinnamon apple pie or peanut butter and jelly ice cream.

And that's just the *first* choice you have to make.

Next, you have to pick a cone, and that's a lot of pressure to put on a kid! Do you like regular, sugar, waffle, honey-dipped, or chocolate with nuts? They even have a bowl made out of a cone.

But then you *still* have to pick your toppings. Do you want whipped cream, hot fudge, butterscotch, cookie pieces, cherries, marshmallows, or mini peanut butter cups?

It's enough to make any kid feel a little dizzy!

That's why I like to keep things simple. I always order the same thing: two scoops of vanilla on a sugar cone. No toppings.

I know, I know. You're thinking that's a really normal, boring type of ice-cream cone, but there's a reason for that.

One time I tried a new kind of ice-cream cone, and things got out of hand . . . *fast!*

That's me, Andres Miedoso. I'm the one covered in an ice-cream tidal wave while slipping off a diving board.

And there's Desmond Cole, my best friend. He's the one using a sticky caramel rope to save me from falling.

DESMOND COLE

And no, your eyes are not playing tricks on you. That *is* a giant ice-cream-cone monster chasing us. His name is the I Scream Man.

And let's just say that he's very, very hungry!

ANDRES MIEDOSO

CHAPTER TWO

PLAIN OLD VANILLA

Wait. I don't want to get ahead of myself. Let's start at the beginning.

It was a *hot* summer in Kersville. Yeah, I know summer is *always* hot, but it felt like you were standing on the sun.

That's how hot it was!

All the lakes went dry. Kids got sunburns in the shade. Bike tires were melting on the street, and there was only one place we wanted to be: the Kersville Pool!

I'm telling you—everybody was there.

The pool was so packed that you could hardly find space to swim. And if you wanted to get on a diving board, you had to wait in a long line.

No, thanks.

Desmond and I just wanted to spend as much time as we could cooling off in the water. And that's exactly what we did.

It was perfect . . . until we got kicked out for something called "Adult Swim."

Adult Swim was a time when kids had to leave the sweet coolness of the pool so grown-ups could have a turn. I guess grown-ups can't swim so good, or maybe they need more room or something.

Either way, it was super-mean to make us leave the pool right when the sun sizzled kids to a crisp.

There was one good thing about Adult Swim. It was our chance to visit the Itsy-Bitsy Ice Cream truck!

Talk about a blast of chilly, yummy goodness! As soon as Desmond and I heard the cheerful music, we forgot about those silly grown-ups. I mean, is there anything better than an ice-cream truck on a hot summer day?

Of course not!

We did what kids do when they hear that music. We ran!

But no matter how fast we moved, there was a line of kids already there.

The Itsy-Bitsy Ice Cream truck had everything a kid could want. They had bubble gum, lollipops, and gummies in flavors like sweet, sour, and even *totally gross*.

There were candy bars, *frozen* candy bars, shaved ice, and a million kinds of Popsicles.

Desmond and I came for the ice cream, though. They had the regular flavors all the time, but there were super-crazy flavors to pick from too.

While we waited in line, Desmond studied the menu on the side of the truck and read all the ice-cream flavors.

CORN BREAD *and* BACON

SALT *and* PEPPER

GREEN TEA *and* PICKLE JUICE

MACARONI *and* CHEESE CURLS

ALL CHARMS, NO CEREAL

SPICY TAFFY *with* HOT CHIPS

CARROT *with* MAPLE SYRUP

"These sound so *weird!*" Desmond said. "I want to try each one!"

When we finally got to the front of the line, we waved hello to Anthony. He owned the Itsy-Bitsy Ice Cream truck. Desmond and I met him because of a werewolf, but that's another story.

"Hey, Anthony. Hot enough for ya?" Desmond asked.

Anthony smiled and said, "It's so hot that I can't even make a *chilly* dog!"

Desmond and I laughed. Anthony had a zillion bad jokes.

"Okay, I'm ready," Desmond said. "May I please have two big scoops of macaroni-and-cheese-curls ice cream in a chocolate-dipped waffle cone with pretzel bits and rainbow sprinkles on top?"

"Coming right up!" Anthony said.
"You order the most creative things, Desmond," I said as Anthony handed Desmond his cone.

Once Desmond had his treat, Anthony turned to me and asked, "Do you want the usual, Andres?"

I nodded. Even though my order wasn't as fun as Desmond's, it was still cool that Anthony knew my order by heart.

"One plain old vanilla cone coming right up," said Anthony.

CHAPTER THREE

SUGAR CONES

Eating ice cream made the world seem perfect again.

Suddenly, Adult Swim was almost over, and the sun slipped behind a cloud, so the air cooled down enough that we stopped sweating.

Life was good.

Plus, the ice cream was delicious, as always! Nothing could ruin the moment.

Well, almost nothing.

After the last kid was served, Anthony leaned out the window of his truck.

"Kids, I have an announcement," he said. "Starting tomorrow I'm going on vacation, so I won't see you for a week."

All of our jaws dropped at the same exact time!

"Oh no," said a girl.
"What are we going
to do?" a boy asked.
"Don't
leave,"
begged
another girl.
Even Desmond
looked shocked.
"A whole week without
ice cream?"
And I got so mad
that I screamed the first
thing that came to mind.
"Oh sugar cones!"

"I know," Desmond agreed. Then he said, "Wait, did you say 'sugar cones'?"

I shrugged. "Give me a break. I was upset, and I didn't know what else to say."

Desmond shook his head. "Sometimes you're really strange, Andres Miedoso."

We both laughed, and it felt good. Then we heard Anthony start up the truck.

"Wait!" Desmond called out. "You can't leave us for a whole week without any ice cream."

"Sorry, Desmond," Anthony said. "It's only a week. I'm sure you'll survive."

And with that, the Itsy-Bitsy Ice Cream truck pulled away, taking our joy with it. Nothing would be the same at the pool without the world's best ice cream.

Just then the lifeguard blew her whistle. Adult Swim was over, and kids could go back into the pool.

For a second it felt like everything was going to be fine.

Oh, but it wouldn't be fine. Not even close.

CHAPTER FOUR

ROCKY ROAD

The next day Desmond was at my house bright and early.

"I've got a plan to help the ice-cream situation," he said.

Uh-oh. I braced myself because when Desmond Cole has a plan, it can involve just about anything.

But Desmond knows me well. "Don't worry. It's not dangerous. I was thinking that if Anthony won't bring us ice cream next week, then we'll have to make our own."

"Yes!" I cheered.

We went to the kitchen where my parents were having their coffee and checking e-mail.

"Mom and Dad," I began, "do you know how to make ice cream?"

Before they could answer, their laptops beeped loudly. It sounded like hundreds of e-mails were coming in.

"Yikes!" said Dad. "Can we make it tonight? There's a . . . problem at the office."

They didn't have to tell me twice.
See, my parents both work for the
government. Their work is top secret,
so I don't know exactly what they do.
But I know it's important.

Before I could say another word about homemade ice cream, they grabbed their laptops and scrambled out to the car. They didn't even have time to finish their coffee.

"Wow, Andres," Desmond said. "Your parents are so cool!"

"Yeah," I said, "but they're always busy. Sometimes I wish I had regular parents."

"Don't worry," Desmond said. "We can make ice cream on our own. It'll be fun."

"Have you ever made ice cream before?" I asked him.

Desmond smiled. "Nope, but how hard can it be?"

I thought of the flavors Anthony sold and how creamy and yummy they were, and I realized making ice cream *could* be *very* hard.

That's when a ghost flew into the kitchen.

Well, not *any* ghost. It was just Zax. He's the ghost who lives in my house, but that's a whole different story.

"What's up with your parents?"
Zax asked. "They ran so fast that
smoke was coming off their shoes!"

"It's a top secret thing," I told him.
"But Desmond and I have our own
emergency. We want to make ice
cream."

Zax scratched his ghost head. "I thought the Itsy-Bitsy Ice Cream truck had everything."

I filled Zax in on Anthony's vacation and Desmond's plan.

"So you don't want all those kids to be upset," Zax said as he did some quick math. "And to do that you're going to need a bunch of ice cream to keep everybody happy. You're going to need an ice-cream man."

"You're right," Desmond exclaimed.

"It's hopeless," I said.

"Maybe not," said Zax.

Zax put on his thinking face, which is when his eyes look exactly like question marks. It was very weird.

Then his eyes became light bulbs.

"I have an idea," he said. "A buddy of mine can help. We even call him the 'Ice-Cream Man'—he loves making kids scream with joy. Let me see if I can reach him!"

Zax flew out of the room through the wall, and for a few seconds I felt really excited. How cool was it that Zax knew an ice-cream man?

But then I thought about what he said and how he said it.

"Wait, Desmond," I said, suddenly feeling kind of nervous. "Did Zax say 'Ice-Cream Man' or 'I Scream Man'?"

Deep down I think I already knew the answer.

CHAPTER FIVE

THE I SCREAM MAN

The next day was hotter than the day before . . . if that was even possible!

It seemed like the entire town of Kersville was trying to cool down at the pool.

Desmond and I looked for a spot to squeeze into.

We had to hop from one foot to the other because the ground felt like we were walking on hot coals!

Finally we found a place in the kiddie pool—and you know what that means, right? Little kids never leave the water . . . even if they have to go to the bathroom, so Desmond and I had to watch out.

Just when we started to relax, we heard a strange melody ringing out over all the laughing and splashing. The music sounded off-key and kind of haunting.

Everybody in the pool stopped what they were doing to listen.

"What in the world is that sound?" Desmond whispered.

"I'm not sure," I replied. "It sounds like a weird ice-cream truck."

A kid next to me said, "Ice-cream truck?"

Then the rest of the kids yelled, "Ice-cream truck!"

The pool was empty in no time. Everyone ran toward the creepy song—everyone except for Desmond and me.

We had the pool to ourselves, which was awesome. We swam over to the diving boards and took turns jumping into the water.

First we did
cannonballs.
Then we did
can openers.
Then Desmond
started making
up his own dives.
"This is a Monster Claw!"
he said as he jumped
high into the air
with his body
twisted into
the weirdest
position.

Then Desmond climbed up to the high diving board.

"Watch this move," he called down to me. "It's the Mummy Belly Flop!"

Desmond landed with a splash so big that it felt like most of the water flew out of the pool.

We were having so much fun that we didn't think about where the other kids had gone. All I knew was that it was my turn to try the high dive!

Now, this thing was so high, it took forever to climb. I stopped halfway up just to catch my breath.

When I got to the top, I could see the whole town of Kersville. It was quiet . . . too quiet.

I looked down and saw where the kids from the pool went. From way up here, they looked like little ants. But something was definitely wrong.

They weren't moving at all!

I kept staring, and that was when I saw him.

The I Scream Man had arrived.

CHAPTER SIX

LET'S BANANA SPLIT!

"Hey, Andres," Desmond called. "Are you going to jump or what?"

Looking down I remembered something. I am *not* a high-dive guy.

I backed away from the front of the board when a blast of cold air hit me.

"Desmond? Did you feel that?" I yelled while shivering. "There's something strange going on. I'm coming down!"

The chilly wind blew again when I was on the ladder. It was even harder this time, and snowflakes fluttered around me. I caught one on my tongue and realized that these weren't snowflakes.

They were sprinkles . . . rainbow sprinkles!

By the time I got to the ground, I was covered in sprinkles from head to toe!

Desmond swam over to me and climbed out of the pool. "What in the world happened to you?"

I was too sprinkled to talk, so I shook my body like a wet dog, and the candy toppings flew off.

I grabbed Desmond by the arm. "Like I said, something strange is going on. I think it's that new ice-cream man."

We left the pool and found the other kids. They all looked happy . . . a little *too* happy.

Oh, and did I mention *they were all frozen solid?!*

"This is definitely not normal," Desmond whispered.

"Not even in Kersville," I added.

We looked past the kids and saw
an ice-cream truck. But it didn't
look anything like the Itsy-Bitsy Ice
Cream truck. Nope. This truck was
pitch-black and sizzled in the sun.

"Desmond," I whimpered. "I do *not* want ice cream from that truck."

"Wait a minute," he replied. "Let's see what kind of ice cream they have first."

Desmond loves strange things, and that menu was stranger than strange:

MUMMY ICE CREAM *with* **FRESH WORM CHUNKS**

VAMPIRE FANG POPSICLE

BROCCOLI SHERBET *with* **GOBLIN GOO**

GREEN BOOGER SLUSHY

WEREWOLF FUR ICE-CREAM SANDWICH

FROZEN GHOUL YOGURT

ZOMBIE MILKSHAKE *with* **EYEBALLS**

Now I was shivering more than ever!

MUMMY ICE CREAM *with* FRESH W

VAMPIRE FANG POPSI

BROCCOLI SHERBET *with* GOB

GREEN BOOGER SLUSH

WEREWOLF FUR ICE-CREAM SA

FROZEN GHOUL YOGURT

ZOMBIE MILKSHAKE *with* EYE

"Look," Desmond said, pointing to the bottom of the menu. "There's something written in teeny-tiny small print."

He pulled out a magnifying glass.
(And no, I had no idea where he was
keeping it!)

"What does it say?" I asked.

Desmond leaned closer and read,
"It says, 'The price for this ice cream
is—'"

Before Desmond could finish reading, a giant ice-cream-cone monster sprang from the truck window and bellowed, "YOUR *SOUL!*"

CHAPTER SEVEN

CHOCOLATE CHIP COOKIE D'OH!

Have you ever thought about all the different kinds of screams you've heard in your life?

I mean, there are pop-quiz screams and big-bug screams. There are falling-off-your-bike screams and scary-movie screams!

Well, I bet you've never heard the scream from a kid who has come face-to-face with a monster shaped like a giant ice cream without the cone. Trust me—*that* is a scream you would remember!

The I Scream Man was melty in all the wrong places. He reached his ooey-gooey arms out toward us, but Desmond and I were fast. And you would be fast too if a creepy frozen treat tried to grab you.

It was horrible!

Just as the I Scream Man was gaining on us, Desmond said, "I have an idea."

To be honest, the only thing scarier than having the world's biggest ice-cream scoop chasing you is hearing Desmond Cole say he has an idea at a time like that.

Before I could talk him out of his idea, Desmond stopped running and turned to the creamy creature.

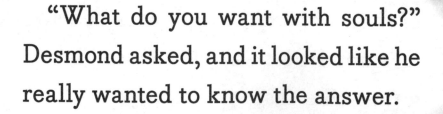

"What do you want with souls?" Desmond asked, and it looked like he really wanted to know the answer.

But the I Scream Man didn't want
to talk. Instead, he started hurling
creepy gummy candy at us.

"Look out, Desmond!" I screamed.

Then, without even thinking about my own safety, I did what any best friend would do: I jumped in front of Desmond and started chomping down on all that candy.

It was a tough job, but someone had to do it!

Also, everything tasted so delicious. It was hard to stop eating it.

The next thing I knew, I was covered in sweets for the second time that day.

Desmond grabbed me and brushed me off.

"How did the candy taste?" he asked me.

"Yummy and haunted," I said kind of dreamily.

I could tell there was a problem. The candy was *too* good. I needed more. In a daze, I raced back to the ice-cream truck. *I have to have more!* But Desmond caught my arm.

"You'll thank me for this later!" he screamed, and we took off running again, with the I Scream Man right behind us!

CHAPTER EIGHT

A Waffle Lot of Danger

We ran back to the pool as scoops of every flavor of ice cream plopped around us. The I Scream Man was pelting us with everything from chocolate chip to strawberry to vanilla, my favorite.

I tried to catch a scoop in my mouth.

Can you blame me? Ice cream is delicious, even if it's served by a haunted ghoul.

Then the ice cream stopped, and something a lot more dangerous and pointy crashed next to us: cones!

All kinds of cones smacked us! Sugar cones, waffle cones, and even those chocolate-dipped waffle cones with those sharp little peanuts stuck to them. And let me tell you—those things *hurt*!

I know you're probably wondering why the adults weren't helping us, but the truth is that they didn't even notice what was happening. Yes, it was Adult Swim again.

They were lying on their backs in the pool or baking in the sun or *whatever* it is that grown-ups do at the pool.

Desmond and I were on our own. So we kept running!

But running at the pool always gets noticed . . . by the lifeguard.

She blew her whistle and said, "Slow down!"

Oh man!

Desmond and I had no choice. We had to stop running. And you'll never believe what happened next. The I Scream Man stopped running too!

I guess *everybody* listens to the lifeguard!

Our high-speed chase turned into a slow-speed walk. That didn't matter, though. The I Scream Man was still hurling treats at us. I guess lifeguards are okay with that.

After a few times around the pool, Desmond said those words again.

"I have an idea, Andres. I bet the I Scream Man won't follow us up the high dive. And if he does, there's no way he'll jump into the pool. I mean, have you ever seen what happens to an ice-cream cone in the pool?"

"It's not pretty," I said, shaking my head.

Okay, I had to admit, Desmond's idea wasn't bad. Plus, it was the only idea we had, so we headed for the high-dive ladder.

And just like Desmond thought, the I Scream Man didn't follow us. He stayed down by the pool and kept up his ice-cream attack. Once we reached the top, I got pummeled with a scoop of rainbow sherbet, which tasted great but knocked me off-balance.

Luckily, Desmond pulled on a long drip of caramel sauce and made it into a rope. He wrapped it around my waist as I teetered back and forth. Then Desmond said the three words you should never say to someone on the edge of a diving board that high in the air.

"Don't look down."

Well, I did what anybody would do in that situation. I looked down.

And boy, was that a *huge* mistake. The height made my belly gurgle really, really bad. Maybe I shouldn't have eaten all that sugar, but it tasted so good.

I couldn't help myself. I took one more bite . . . of the caramel rope.

And that was how I took my first jump off the high dive.

CHAPTER NINE

It Was Mint to Be

What happened next? Well, let's just say I made a big splash.

First, there was my belly flop, which was bigger than Desmond's had been earlier. My belly flop was so powerful that it sent most of the adults flying out of the pool.

Next, all that sugary sweetness in my belly decided to . . . Um, how should I say this? It came back out, just like a geyser, right there in the pool.

Just thinking about it makes me feel kind of *green* inside because I wasn't the only one who got sick.

The grown-ups got sick next.

Then the lifeguard.

And then . . . I know you're not going to believe me, but it's true. The I Scream Man got sick too! Ugh.

Watching a giant ice-cream man getting sick is something you don't want to see. Take my word for it! It's something you will never be able to unsee no matter how hard you try.

And I tried!

There were only two folks who didn't get sick that day: Desmond, and Zax, who had floated to the pool with a smile on his face.

"Hey, guys," Zax said. "Did my friend help out with the I Scream? I mean, isn't he the scariest I Scream Man you've ever seen?"

"Zax!" Desmond cried. "We wanted ice cream." Then he spelled it out for Zax. *"I-C-E C-R-E-A-M!* We didn't want something that was going to scare the insides out of us!"

Zax looked a little embarrassed.

"Oops. I'm sorry. I thought that being scared made kids happy. They always scream with delight."

I swam to the edge of the pool, through all the, um, globs, and climbed out. I didn't want Zax to feel bad.

"Kids do like scary stories," I explained. "But that doesn't mean we like to be chased by haunted ice-cream cones! We just want to eat ice-cream cones."

"Okay," Zax said, nodding. "I think I get it now."

Just then the I Scream Man came over with a big frown on his face. "Zax, pal. You told me the kids would love it if I made them scream."

Desmond smiled. "Actually, the kids would love it if you made them *ice cream!*"

The I Scream Man thought about that for a few seconds. "So you want me to make the kids *into* ice cream?"

"NO!" Desmond and I yelled at the same time.

"Can you just *give* the kids ice cream for free?" I asked. "Because you scared them stiff already!"

The I Scream Man nodded.

"Serving ice cream, huh? That sounds fun. Why didn't I think of that in the first place?" he said.

"Maybe, umm, because you're a monster?" Desmond suggested.

"Oh yeah!" the I Scream Man said. Zax looked happy too. "Hey, I was just trying to help. But I guess ghosts aren't always good at understanding humans."

You can say that again, I thought.

CHAPTER TEN

THE INSIDE SCOOP

POOL CLOSED
FOR
CLEANING

They had to close the pool for the day, which was fine with us kids because that pool was gross.

The rest of the week was great, though. The I Scream Man came back to the pool every day, and he gave us all free ice cream!

He still had weird flavors, but not scary ones. And guess what? I tried some new flavors.

I guess even a plain-vanilla-cone guy needs something new every now and then! And who knew that chocolate-covered lemon sherbet with marshmallow-butterscotch swirl would be so yummy?

And I know what you're thinking: What happened when Anthony came back from his vacation?

Well, guess what? Anthony and the I Scream Man teamed up. They work together now with *two ice-cream trucks*. That means the lines move twice as fast!

In fact, the I Scream Man invented a special new kind of ice cream that mixed sweet treats with balloons. He called them "Ice-Cream Floats"!

You know that it was Desmond's favorite.

And best of all, if we ever needed to end Adult Swim early, the I Scream Man was there to help us out.

Let's just say he's our scary super-scooper secret with grown-up screams on top!